minedition

published by Michael Neugebauer Publishing Ltd. Hong Kong

distributed in GB by BOUNCE! Sales and Marketing Ltd, London

Text and Illustrations copyright © 2009 by Ayano Imai

Original title: Puss & Boots

English text adaption by Kate Westerlund

Coproduction with Michael Neugebauer Publishing Ltd., Hong Kong.

Rights arranged with "minedition" Rights and Licensing AG, Zurich, Switzerland.

Manufactured in China.

Typesetting in Papyrus for headlines and Nueva by Carol Twombly for text

Colour separation by HiFai, Hong Kong

A CIP Catalogue record for this book is available from the British Library

ISBN 978-988-97794-7-4

10 9 8 7 6 5 4 3 2

Second Impression

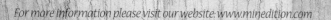

For more information please visit our website: www.minedition.com

Puss & Boots

by Ayano Imai

Translated from the Japanese
by Sayako Uchida

Adapted by

Kate Westerlund

minedition

There once was a poor shoemaker who lived with his cat. Business was not good, and as they shared the last can of tuna the shoemaker said, "Cat, I'm afraid that's it. We're finished! There are no more orders. I guess I will have to look for a new job."

"Perhaps you give up too easily," said the cat. "Make me a pair of your most beautiful boots and I will go as your messenger and find new orders for you!"

And that is exactly what happened…

The cat put on the beautiful new boots and went out prepared to get enough orders so the shoemaker would be busy and become successful.

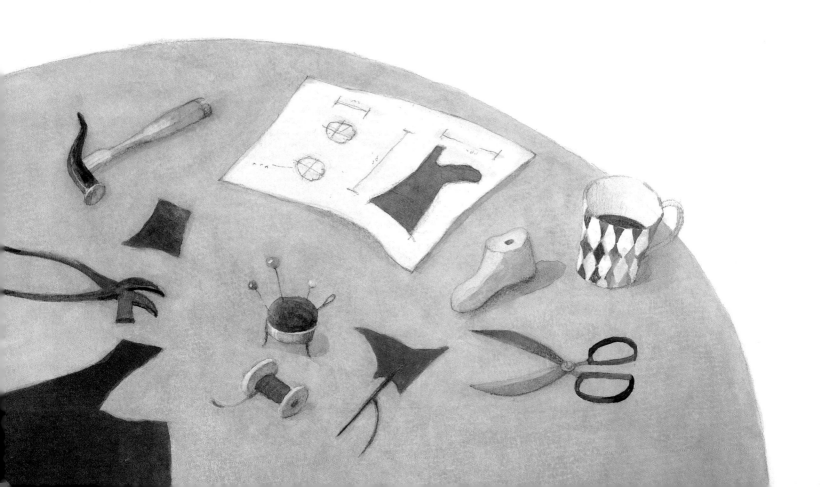

Deep in the woods the cat came upon a magnificent castle.
It was said that the castle belonged to a terrible monster.
This monster had a magical power — he could change
himself into any form he wanted.

The cat met the monster and introduced himself as a messenger from the best shoemaker in the land.

"I have heard," said the cat, "that you can transform yourself into anything you wish. Someone with such incredible talent and power surely must need shoes of equal quality."

When the monster saw the beautiful boots the cat was wearing, he knew he must have shoes that were just as beautiful. So he ordered a pair for himself.

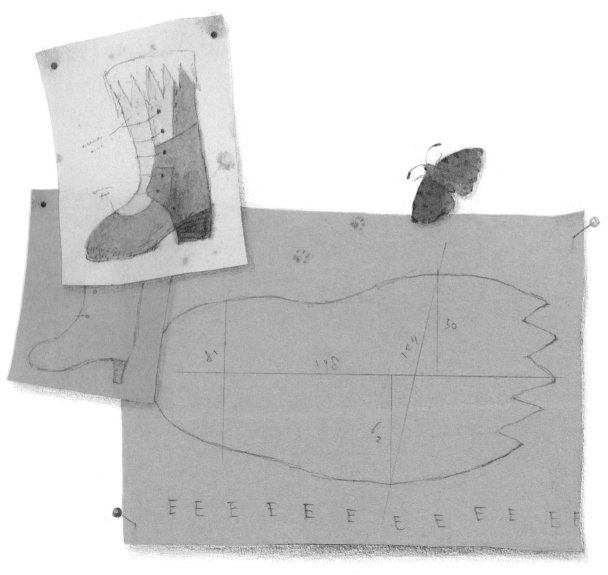

When the cat presented the finished shoes, the monster realized he must have the right shoes to match each creature he turned himself into.
He ordered one pair of shoes after the other.

The cat came regularly to the castle to measure
the monster's feet and to deliver the finished shoes.
Each pair seemed more beautiful than the one before.
The monster was delighted. There was just one problem.
The monster was rich, but he was also a miserly,
stingy old tightwad of a monster.

When the cat asked for payment, the monster turned himself into a frightening wild beast and said, "I am a great and powerful monster. The shoes are mine, I will not pay!"

And he chased the cat from the castle.

But the clever cat had a plan.

He asked the shoemaker to make a very special pair of shoes.

When they were finished he went back to the castle to show them to the monster.

"The shoemaker has outdone himself," said the cat. "He has made a pair of the finest shoes I have ever seen. They are of materials so rare and valuable that only someone with your great-ness should have them. But the shoes are so tiny that I doubt even you, with your great power, could change yourself into something so small. Why, you would have to be the size of say, well…

a tiny mouse, for instance."

"Ho, ho," said the monster. "You just watch me!"
And with a great roar and a puff of smoke, the monster turned himself into a tiny mouse.
"You see, I'm exactly the right size," said the monster and started to put on the beautiful shoes.

"You certainly are," said the cat and he pounced on the mouse and gobbled him up.

The shoemaker and his trusty cat moved into the castle and opened up a wonderful new shop.

The townspeople had always feared the monster.
They couldn't imagine why he had left.
But they soon stopped being afraid and began buying their shoes from the shoemaker again.

There was another curious thing.
No one seemed able to explain who would ever be able to wear the odd collection of shoes on display in the window – particularly a beautiful little pair, hardly big enough for a mouse.

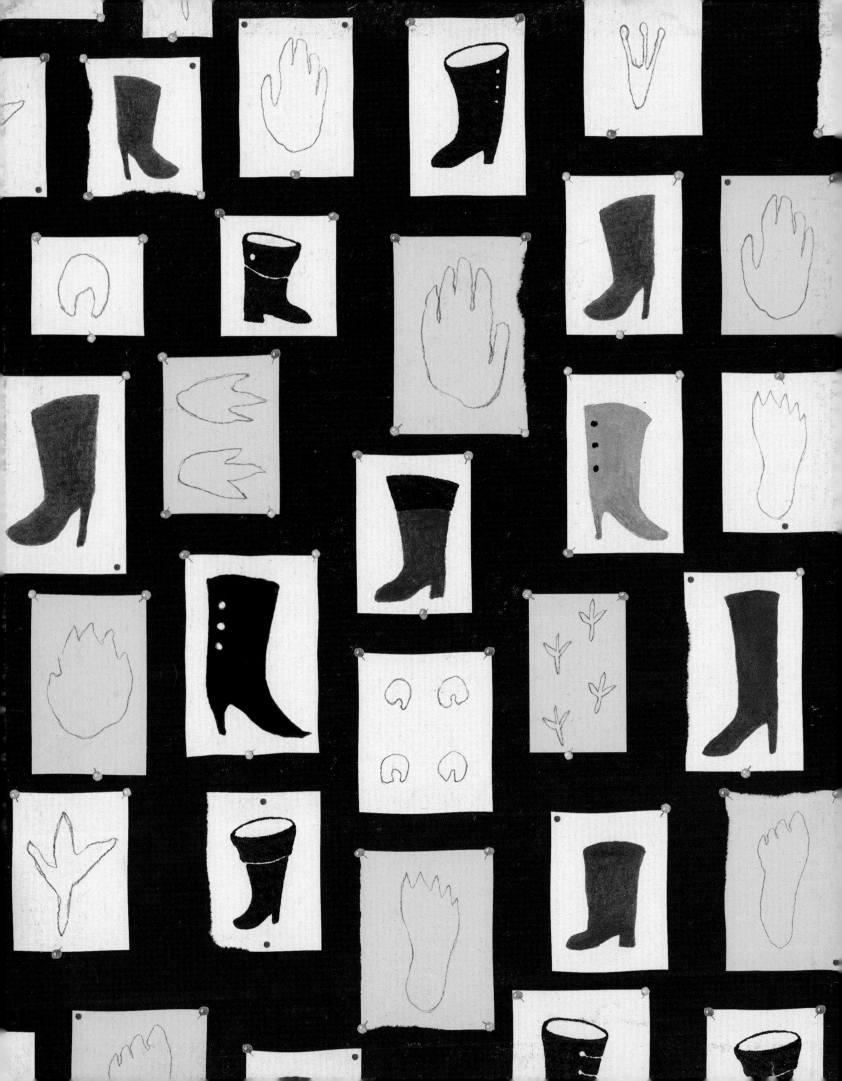